Goosebumps
Haunted Halloween
SLAPPY'S RETURN

ADAPTED BY KATE HOWARD

BASED ON THE MOTION PICTURE

GOOSEBUMPS: HAUNTED HALLOWEEN

WRITTEN BY ROB LIEBER

GOOSEBUMPS and associated logos are registered trademarks of Scholastic Inc.
© 2018 Columbia Pictures Industries, Inc. All Rights Reserved.

Published by Scholastic Inc., *Publishers since 1920.* SCHOLASTIC and
associated logos are trademarks and/or registered trademarks of Scholastic Inc.

ISBN 978-1-338-31570-7

10 9 8 7 6 5 4 3 2   18 19 20 21 22

Printed in the U.S.A.   40

First printing 2018

The town of Wardenclyffe was ready for H
Yards were full of ghosts, zombies, skeletons, and giant
But Sonny Quinn couldn't enjoy the spooky holiday
too busy with his science project. He was building a min
of Nikola Tesla's Wardenclyffe Lab. It would be amazin
could ever get it to work.

Sonny adjusted the wires on his model. The next mon
the lights in the house went out.

"Sonny, please stop electrocuting yourself," called his mom, Kathy. "Come finish your breakfast."

"Sorry, Mom," Sonny said.

Sonny's sister, Sarah, stomped down the stairs. "This is the fifth time this month you've blown the fuse!" Her hair looked crazy—her blow-dryer had lost power.

"Get your backpacks on," Kathy told the kids. "I have to stop by the drugstore on the way to school."

Sonny's friend Sam ran through the Quinns' front door. He was carrying a suitcase. "Good morning, Mrs. Quinn."

Sam's dad waved to Kathy from outside in his car. "Thanks so much for taking Sam—we'll be back in three days. We owe you!" he called.

Kathy smiled. "You definitely do." She turned to the three kids. "All right, let's go!"

At the drugstore, Sam pulled a flyer out of his backpack. It said: "Got junk? Call THE JUNK BROS — the best in junk removal."

"Why do you say we're brothers?" Sonny asked as Sam taped the flyer to the store's bulletin board.

Sam grinned. "Because we're basically brothers. And studies show that four out of five people trust family businesses."

Sarah followed her mom through the store.

"Sarah," Kathy said. "I need you to watch Sonny and Sam this week. I have to work double shifts."

"Mom, are you kidding?" Sarah asked. "Sonny's thirteen! He's old enough to watch himself."

Kathy raised her eyebrows. "He blows up his science projects even when I'm home. Imagine what he'd get up to if we leave him home alone."

That afternoon, Sonny and Sam got their first Junk Bros job. The two boys rode their bikes over to 24 Ashley Lane. They were going to clear out an old house.

A faded name on the mail slot said: *Stine*. The front porch was run-down and crowded with creepy garden gnomes.

"I don't like the way those things are looking at us," Sonny said.

Sonny knocked, and the door creaked open.

Inside, the house was a mess. There were piles of broken lamps, old mattresses, and papers.

"How much are they paying us for this?" Sonny asked.

Sam bit his lip. "Well, the lady said we can keep any junk we don't throw away . . ."

"You told them we'd work for free?" Sonny yelled. He sighed. Then he noticed an old wooden crate behind the fireplace. Inside was a dusty, leather-bound manuscript.

"It's just an old book," Sonny said, paging through it.

Sam tossed the book into a box of things to keep. "The cover might get us a few bucks."

"Sam . . ." Sonny said, turning around slowly. "That wasn't there before, was it?"

A wooden ventriloquist dummy with a frozen smile was now sitting in the crate. Sonny pulled a piece of paper out of the dummy's pocket.

" 'Hi. My name's Slappy. What's yours?' " he read aloud.

"There's more on the back," Sam told him.

Sonny flipped the paper over. "*Karru Marri Odonna Loma Molonu Karrano* . . . I think it's another language."

Sam frowned at the dummy. "So creepy. He looks alive . . ."

Sonny and Sam tossed everything into their wagons. Then they started biking home.

But they didn't get far. A kid from school, Tommy Madigan, and his bully friends blocked their path.

"Hey, stop!" Tommy called out. "Give me those boxes . . . unless you want your face punched."

"No way," Sam said. "We worked for this stuff."

Tommy just laughed. He grabbed the dummy and the book.

As soon as the words came out of his mouth, Tommy's pants fell down. "What?" he said, tugging them back up.

While Tommy was distracted, Sam grabbed Slappy away from him.

"Sonny, let's go!" Sam said, forgetting about the book.

Tommy screamed, "I'm going to get you for this, Sam!"

Sam and Sonny pedaled away as fast as they could. But Tommy and his crew were gaining on them.

Back inside the wagon, Slappy glared at Tommy and his gang. Suddenly, *FWAP!* A garden hose flew out of a front yard, knocking Tommy and his friends off their bikes.

"That was awesome!" Sam cheered.

Sonny grinned at Slappy. "He's like our good luck charm."

That night, Sonny practiced his presentation in front of Slappy.
"Nikola Tesla wanted to transmit everything through electric towers—power, sound, maybe even brain waves!" he began. "After Tesla shut down his lab, his tower never lit up the sky again. Until today! I will use the power inside my tower to light this bulb from across the room."

He placed a light bulb in Slappy's lap. Then he touched two wires together. Nothing happened.

"Come on," Sonny growled. "Can't this work, just once?"

"Bravo!" said a voice. It was coming from Slappy!
"It's an electrifying presentation."

Sonny looked around in surprise. "I'm not falling for that trick, Sam," he said.

Slappy blinked. "You brought me to life. Don't you remember, Sonny?"

Sonny backed away. The dummy . . . was talking! "How are you speaking to me right now?" he asked.

"I've always wanted a brother," Slappy said.

"Sam!" Sonny yelled down the stairs. "Get up here. Now!"

"Hello, Sam," Slappy said. "Thank you for saving me today. Now that we're family, we can be brothers."

Sam whispered, "Are we losing our minds?"

Sonny shook his head. "I don't think we can both lose our minds at the same time. Maybe he's real . . . ?"

Slappy giggled. "Of course I'm real."

Slappy began moving things around the room—without using his hands.

"Oh my goodness," Sam said. "You can move things with your mind?"

Slappy nodded. "Whatever I see, I can bring to life. I can make your problems go away—like I did with Tommy today. *Karru Marri Odonna Loma Molonu Karrano . . .*"

"Wait till Sarah and my mom see this!" Sam whooped.

"Let's keep this our little secret for now," Slappy said.

Late that night, while everyone was asleep, Slappy got to work.

He had always wanted a family. Now that he had found one, he would do whatever it took to make his new brother love him. So he made a few adjustments to Sonny's science project.

There, Slappy thought with a grin. *That should help . . .*

The next day, Sonny presented his project to the class.

"Behold," Sonny said, handing one of his classmates a bare light bulb. "I will light this bulb from across the room with the power inside my tower."

Sonny clicked a switch to ON. Electricity crackled as his model came to life. Power waves shot through the air, lighting the bulb. The light grew brighter and brighter.

Suddenly, a bolt of lightning shot out of the tower. The light bulb burst. The kids in Sonny's class hid under their desks.

"Sonny blew up the science wing today!" Sam told Sarah when she came to pick up the boys after school.

"It was an accident," Sonny said.

But his sister wanted an answer, so Sonny told her about Slappy, even though he knew it sounded crazy.

Sarah gripped the steering wheel. "Let me get this straight: You discovered a walking, talking dummy and you didn't tell me?!"

"Slappy told us to keep it a secret," Sonny said.

"Sonny, when a doll comes alive and tells you to keep secrets, that's a red flag," Sarah snapped.

Sam held up a hand. "He's more than just a doll. He's got powers. He can move things with his mind."

"Sonny, this is insane!" Sarah said.

"You have to believe me," Sonny said. "He told us he wanted to be a part of the family!"

Back at the Quinns' house, the kids raced inside to find Slappy. They found him sitting on Kathy's lap.

"Hey, kids," Kathy said in a silly voice. "My name is Bobo and I like listening to Mom!"

"Actually, his name is Slappy," Sonny said. "And I wouldn't do that if I were you . . . we found that dummy in an abandoned house—"

"And he came to life," Sam said, cutting him off. "And now he's . . . doing things."

Just then, the phone rang. Kathy jumped up to get it. As soon as Kathy was gone, Slappy came to life. "Hi, kids. Good days at school?"

Sarah stepped back. "He is so creepy," she whispered. Slappy cocked his head. "I'm getting to know Mama. I think she likes me! We're going to be such a happy family. You brought me to life. Now we're together . . . *forever*."

"We're not your family, Slappy," Sarah said. "Turn him off, Sonny."

"Hearing you say that makes me sad," Slappy said.

Sonny repeated the chant that brought Slappy to life. "*Karru, Mari, Ordonna, Madra . . .*"

Slappy's eyes drifted closed, as if he were going to sleep.

"It worked," Sam cheered.

Slappy's eyes popped open again. "And when I get sad . . . I get ery, very MAD!"

Kathy stormed back into the room. Slappy froze in place.

"That was school calling!" Kathy shouted. "You blew up the science lab?!"

"It wasn't Sonny's fault," Sarah said.

"He did it!" Sam said, pointing at Slappy.

"The *dummy* did it?" Kathy asked. "Do *I* look like a dummy to you? Halloween is canceled for the three of you. No costumes. No trick-or-treating. I am so disappointed in you."

As soon as their mom left for work, Sarah dragged her brother and Sam up to her room. "We've got a problem," she said. "We need to get rid of Slappy right away."

Sarah's bedroom door flew open. Slappy stood in the doorway, his face filled with rage. "Did somebody call a family meeting . . . without *me*? This is *my* house now."

"Sorry, Slappy," Sarah said, grabbing a baseball bat from her closet. "You just got voted out of this family."

Sarah stuffed Slappy inside a suitcase, locked it, and tossed the case in the back of her car. Then she and the boys drove to the town swamp.

"We killed a puppet," Sonny said as Sarah tied a heavy dumbbell to the suitcase and threw it into the swamp.

"We had to do it," Sarah said, getting back in the car. "Don't worry about anything, okay? He's in a locked suitcase."

Just then, there was a loud thump on the car roof. Slappy's face leered at them through the windshield. "*SLAPPY'S NOT HAPPY!*"

Sarah swerved the car, trying to throw Slappy off the car. "What do you want from us?" she yelled.

"I just want to be part of the family!" Slappy cried.

Sarah turned the wheel to the right—hard. The car skidded off the road and slammed into a tree.

"Everybody okay?" Sarah asked.

The boys both nodded.

"Where's Slappy?" Sam asked, looking around. There was no sign of the dummy.

Sonny shook his head. "I think we just made things worse."

27

"Okay," Sarah said as soon as they got home. "We need to do some research on dummy attacks." They started to search the Internet.

"Here's a story from 2015," Sonny said, reading aloud. " 'A mysterious disturbance in Madison, Delaware . . . giant insects, abominable snowmen, and even an evil dummy.' " Sarah read over his shoulder. " 'Creatures believed to exist only in the books of horror author R.L. Stine. Some witnesses say the creatures came alive out of the books!' "

Sonny's eyes got wide. "The book! When we found Slappy, there was this old book and we opened it!"

"Where is it now?" Sarah asked.

"Tommy took it," Sam said.

Sonny quickly did another search. " 'From 1979 to 1985,' " he read aloud, " 'horror author R.L. Stine lived in Wardenclyffe . . . He wrote an unpublished novel called *Slappy Halloween*. It's a tale of an evil dummy who sets out to create a family of his own . . . by bringing Halloween to life.' "

"Wait!" Sam said suddenly. "I found a number for Richard Shivers, the president of the R.L. Stine Society."

"It's worth a try," said Sonny.

Sarah called him, but it went straight to voice mail. "Hi, Mr. Shivers," she said. "We need to get in touch with R.L. Stine. We're in Wardenclyffe, New York. And this is going to sound crazy, but . . . I think one of his early stories has come to life. . . ."

After she hung up, Sarah grabbed her jacket. "We need to get that book back—now."

In downtown Wardenclyffe, Slappy was putting his plan into action. He strolled through the Halloween section at a local store.

"Hello, old friends," he said, greeting the costumes. "If those kids don't want me in their family, I'll raise a family of my own." Slappy closed his eyes and began his chant.

"Karru Marri Odonna . . ."

One by one, the costumes came to life.

When a store manager peeked around the corner, Slappy threw an ogre mask at him. The mask latched on to the man's face, and he transformed into an ogre.

Slappy grinned. "Welcome to the family."

Next, Slappy headed for the abandoned Tesla lab. "Why settle for a small family when we can project my power *everywhere* and bring the whole *town* to life?"

Inside the tower, Slappy glanced at the lab's control panel, and it whirred to life. "*Karru Marri* ..." he chanted.

The tower crackled and shot a bolt of electricity across the sky.

"Get me the book," Slappy told the ogre. "And get me Mama."

As they raced toward Tommy's house, Sarah, Sam, and Sonny saw that Halloween decorations had started to come to life all over town.

Garden gnomes were transformed into ghoulish Halloween gnomes. The faces on trick-or-treaters' candy bags came alive. Three witches flew out of the sky and grabbed Tommy and his friends off the street, dragging them into the air.

"Oh no," Sarah said. "We've got to find that book!"

At Tommy's house, Sonny peeked in the front window. Tommy's grandma was sound asleep on the couch, and didn't wake up when they knocked.

"You guys sneak in," Sarah said. "Go find the book. I'll stay out here on lookout."

Sam and Sonny tiptoed through Tommy's house.

"Found it!" Sonny cried. He glanced at the faded leather cover. "R.L. Stine . . . ?"

As he cracked it open, the lights in the house flickered. "Let's go!"

As they raced for the door, Sam took some gummy bears from a bowl of candy. But when he tried to pull his hand back, something grabbed his arm and held on.

"The fake hand inside this candy bowl . . . has my hand!" Sam shrieked.

"Sam . . . " Sonny said, his eyes wide. "Turn around—very slowly."

Sam turned. The gummy bears had come to life!

"Awww," Sam said. "Hi there, little guys."

"You just *ate* their brothers and sisters," Sonny pointed out.

While Sam and Sonny were fighting the gummy bear army, Sonny's cell phone rang. "Mom?" Sonny said. "Help! We're under attack!"

"Sonny, what are you talking about?" Kathy asked. "Put Sarah on the phone!"

Before Sonny could reply, a gummy bear jumped on his head.

"Do not leave the house!" Kathy ordered. "I'm coming home!"

A bear lunged at Sonny, and he held up the only thing he had to protect himself: the book. As the bear reached for Sonny, the book fell open.

WHOOSH! The bear got sucked up into the book!

Sonny gasped. The *book* was a *weapon*.

Holding the book open wide, Sonny aimed it at more gummy bears. The book sucked them all up like a vacuum cleaner.

"Best book ever," Sam said, amazed.

Outside, Sarah was getting impatient. "What are you guys doing in there?"

Sonny shoved the window open, and he and Sam crawled out. "Just being mauled by my favorite comfort food," Sam squeaked.

"Sarah," Sonny panted. "Everything's alive. I mean, even candy! But there's something you need to know about this book . . . it's not normal!"

A zombie bride lurched toward them. Sonny held the book open and showed off the book's amazing power.

"We need to read that book and see how we can end this!" Sarah said. She read aloud, " 'Slappy was a lonely dummy who wanted a family of his own. His revenge was to create a family by bringing Halloween to life. But that wasn't enough, because Slappy wanted more than just a family. He wanted a mother. So his plan was to . . .' "

Sarah looked up. "That's the last page. It's an unfinished manuscript."

"Slappy's going to go after Mom!" Sarah said. "This book is the only thing that can stop him."

"Mom's on her way home to save us!" Sonny said.

Sam took a deep breath. "We need to find your mom before Slappy does."

The three kids raced home. In their neighbor's yard, all the Halloween decorations had come alive. Bedsheet ghosts zipped through the air. Carved pumpkins shot seeds like missiles. A giant balloon spider was casting webs at kids.

"There's Mom!" Sonny said, pointing. "Stuck up in the tree!"

"Give me the book," Sarah said. "You guys get a ladder. Meet me at that tree!"

Sarah raced toward her mom. But a ghost swooped in and knocked the book out of Sarah's hand.

The creature grabbed the book and flew away. Sonny and Sam joined Sarah just in time to see a giant spider pluck Kathy out of the tree. The spider leaped across rooftops with Kathy in its arms.

Across town, Tesla Tower was all lit up.

"Slappy must have brought the tower to life," Sonny said, pointing. "He's using the lab to power Halloween. If we can get inside the tower and find the power source, I can turn it off. Then we can save Mom."

"One problem," Sam said. "There are monsters everywhere. How are we gonna get past them?"

Sarah's eyes lit up. "It's Halloween. Camouflage time!"

Inside Tesla's lab, Slappy was very happy. The spider had delivered Kathy, and the ghost had brought him the book. Everything was going according to plan.

"Hello, Mama," Slappy said. "Remember me?"

When Sarah, Sam, and Sonny raced into the lab, Slappy greeted them. "Isn't this nice? A family reunion," he said, pointing to Kathy. "Do you see my first great invention? I call her Mama."

Sam was horrified. "He turned your mom into a ventriloquist dummy!"

"Turn our mom back now!" Sonny demanded.

"Don't you mean *our* mom?" Slappy said. "Now that my family is complete, I'm going to make certain it's never taken from me again. I'm finally going to do what Stine couldn't. I'm going to finish this book . . . and write an ending that *never ends*. I'll destroy this manuscript and make Halloween last forever!"

Slappy began climbing to the top of the tower. Sarah went after him.

When he reached the tower's highest platform, Slappy grinned.

"And so Slappy merged science with fiction—destroying the manuscript with the same energy that brought this story to life!" he cackled.

Sarah grabbed for the book. She got hold of it, but she couldn't get it open—Slappy was using his mind power to lock it shut!

"What's the matter?" the dummy giggled. "Writer's block?"

Meanwhile, Sonny was looking at wires in the tower's power room.

"I can't turn it off," he groaned.

"Come on," Sam said. "You're the smartest kid in the seventh grade. Even though you blew up the classroom—"

"That's it!" Sonny exclaimed. "We can't turn it off, but we can turn it *up*. Short out the system. Just like I did in the classroom!"

Together, Sonny and Sam pushed the power levels all the way up. The circuit board overloaded, sending blasts of energy up through the tower.

High up on the roof, Slappy growled, "Don't you know the rules of writing, Sarah? Every story has a beginning, middle, and . . ."

Suddenly, a huge surge of electricity shot up from the lab.

". . . and A TWIST!" Sarah yelled. She kicked Slappy into the electrical current. The dummy was blasted into the sky.

Sarah grabbed for the book and held it up, sucking every last monster back inside.

Sarah hurried back into the lab. Her mom and Sonny and Sam were waiting for her.

"Kids?" Kathy said. "What is going on?"

Just then, a man carrying a typewriter burst in. "I'm here! Don't worry!"

"Are you R.L. Stine?" Sarah asked in surprise.

"Yes! I got your message and I'm here to save you," the man declared. "But now I can see you saved yourselves."

Sarah laughed. "Thanks, Mr. Stine. All that matters is this: Halloween is officially over."